peggy

for Peggy and her feathered friends

All rights reserved. First published in Australia in 2012 by Scholastic Australia.
Published in hardcover in the United States by Clarion Books,
an imprint of Houghton Mifflin Harcourt Publishing Company, 2014.

For information about permission to reproduce selections from this book,
write to trade.permissions@hmhco.com or to Permissions,
Houghton Mifflin Harcourt Publishing Company, 3 Park Avenue,
19th Floor, New York, New York 10016.

www.hmhco.com

The illustrations in this book were done in ink and photo collage.
The text was set in ITC Novarese Std.

The Library of Congress has cataloged the hardcover edition as follows:
Walker, Anna, author, illustrator.
Peggy: a brave chicken on a big adventure / by Anna Walker.
pages cm
"First published in Australia in 2012 by Scholastic Australia."
Summary: "Peggy, a hen, has a life-changing adventure when a gust of wind
drops her in a big city." —Provided by publisher.
[1. Chickens—Fiction. 2. Adventure and adventurers—Fiction.
3. City and town life—Fiction.|1. Title.
PZ7.W15214Peg 2014
|E|—dc23   2013034562

ISBN: 978-0-544-25900-3 hardcover
ISBN: 978-0-544-92819-0 paperback

Manufactured in China
10 9 8 7 6 5 4 3 2 1
4500630268

peggy

A Brave Chicken on a Big Adventure

by anna walker

Houghton Mifflin Harcourt
Boston New York

Peggy lived in a small house on a quiet street.

Every day, rain or shine, Peggy ate breakfast,

played in her yard, and watched the pigeons.

One blustery day, a big gust of wind swept down through the clouds, scooping up leaves, twigs, and . . .

Peggy!

Peggy landed with a soft thud.
She was far from home.
She picked herself up, ruffled her feathers, and went for a walk.

Peggy saw things she had never seen before.

Peggy watched, hopped, jumped, twirled, and tasted.

Woof!

She even found a cozy place to rest that
reminded her of home . . .

Although it was not quite the same.

Peggy missed her home.
She tried asking for directions,
but people found it hard to understand her.

In the rushing crowd, Peggy saw a sunflower like the one in her yard.

She followed the sunflower.

The sunflower sat down, so Peggy sat down too.

Outside began moving. They were speeding away from the tall buildings.

When Peggy looked around, the sunflower was leaving the train.

Peggy hopped out of the train, but the sunflower was gone.
She watched the sky grow darker as clouds rolled by.
The wind was cold.
A flock of birds flew quietly overhead.

It was the pigeons.

The pigeons knew the way back to her yard.

It felt good to be home.

Every day, rain or shine, Peggy ate breakfast,

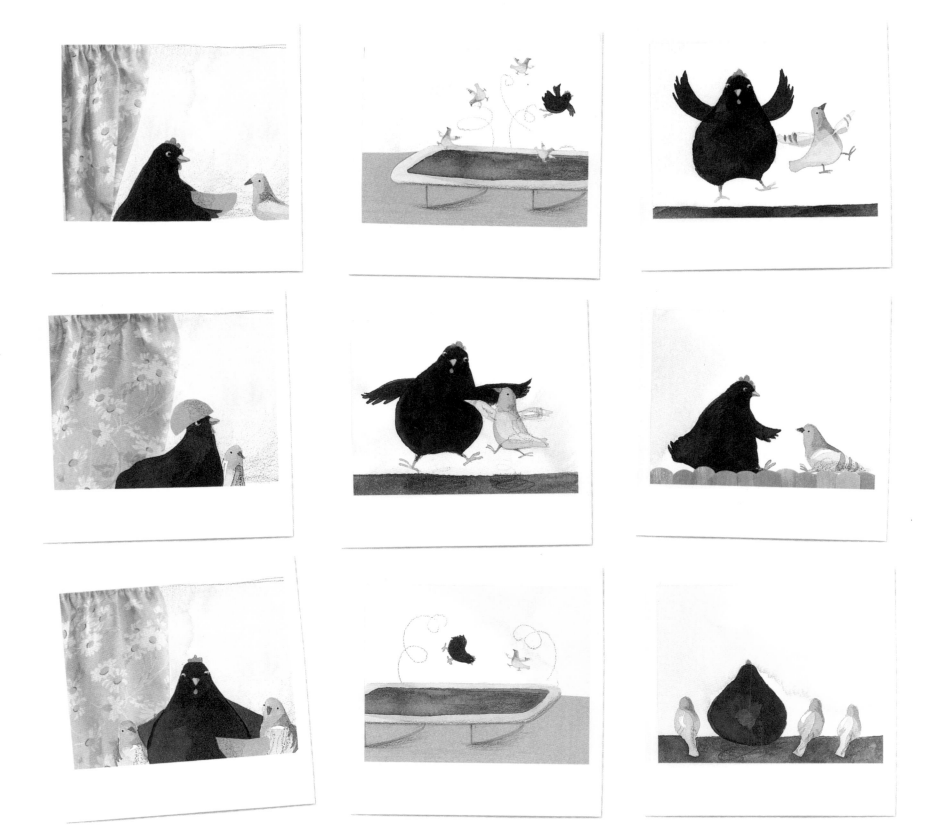

played in her yard, chatted with the pigeons . . .

and sometimes caught the train to the city.

This book belongs to

....

Written by Rosie Greening.
Illustrated by James Dillon.

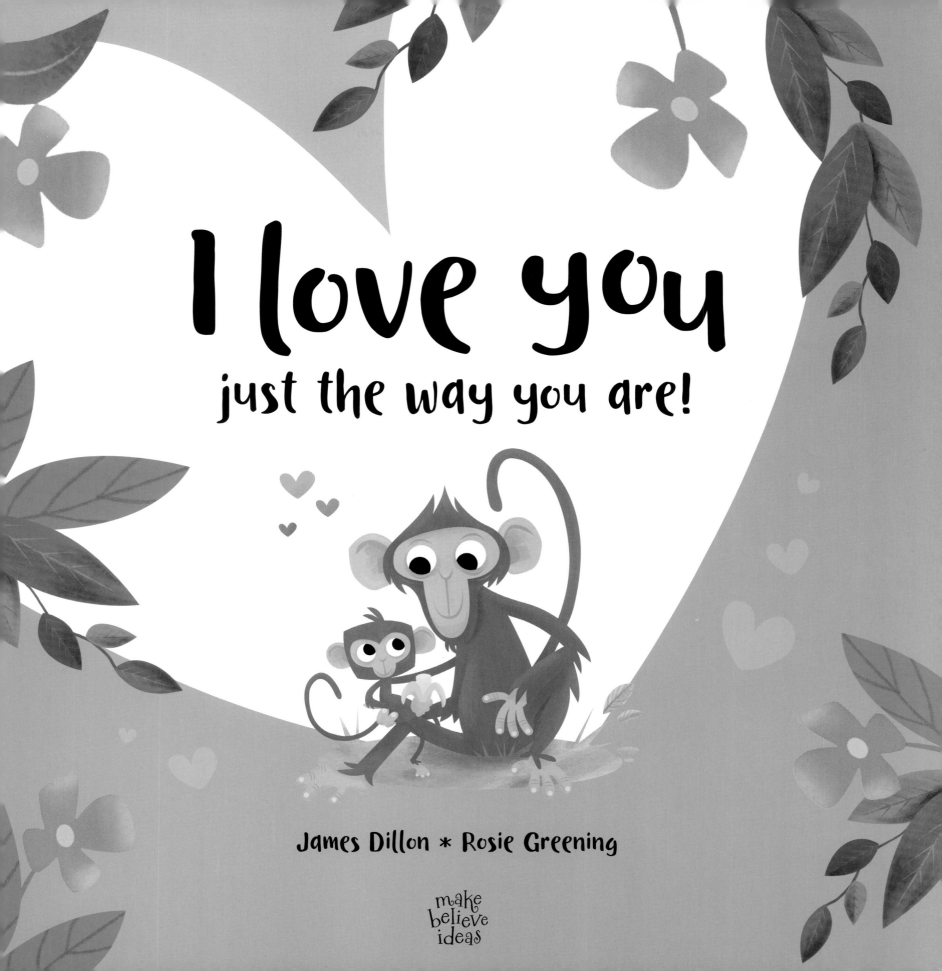

I love you
just the way you are!

James Dillon * Rosie Greening

make
believe
ideas

Each morning,
when I wake you up,
you're

grumpy

as can be.

But you're my dreamy dozer, and that's **alright** with me.

When you're feeling **nervous**, you sometimes try to **hide.**

But **I love you**, timid **turtle**, and I'm **always** by your side.

Even though you're **tiny,** you're the **bravest** mouse I know.

I love you, little **lionheart** –
it's great to watch you **grow**.

You always make

a giant MESS

each time you

eat and play.

Although you are a messy **pup**,
I love you anyway.

You like to **trumpet** loudly, and **stomp** and **stamp** all day.

You're a noisy **elephant**,
but **I love you** that way.

You **scramble** and you **SCURRY**. You **clamber** and you **climb**.

You're my cheeky **monkey** and **I love you** all the time.

Whenever we go **SWIMMING**, you're the splashiest by far.

You're my happy **hippo**
and **I love** how fun you are.

Even when you're **stubborn,**
every day **I love you** more.

When you're in a **prickly** mood,
you **curl** up in a ball.

But you're my spiky **hedgehog**
and **I love you** most of all.

Sometimes you **jump** happily

and **never** want to stop.

You're a fidget, little **frog**,
but **I love** every hop.

Whether you're
red and
angry,

or feeling
down
and **blue,**

I see all your **true colors,**
and the **beauty** inside you.

So remember, in the universe, you are **my** brightest star.

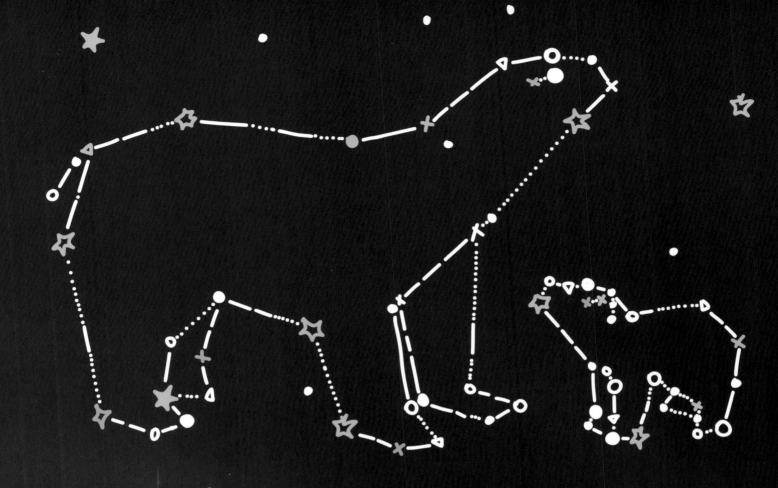

And **no matter what** you say or do, **I love you** as you are!

The End